PRECIOUS MOMENTS®

Sleepy Time
Storybook

PRECIOUS MOMENTS

Sleepy Time Storybook

Samuel J. Butcher, Illustrator
Betty De Vries, Compiler

Baker Books

A Division of Baker Book House Co
Grand Rapids, Michigan 49516

Library of Congress Cataloging-in-Publication Data

Precious moments sleepy time storybook / Samuel J. Butcher, illustrator ; Betty
De Vries, compiler.
    p.   cm.
    Summary: Presents twenty-three stories with a Christian emphasis, deal-
ing with family, identity, and God.
    ISBN 0-8010-4247-X (cloth)
    1. Children's stories, American. [1. Christian life—Fiction. 2. Short stories.]
I. De Vries, Betty. II. Butcher, Samuel J. (Samuel John), 1939–   ill.
PZ5.P7842   1997
[E]—dc21   97-21600

The story written by Marian Schoolland is adapted from *Leading Little Ones to God,*
© 1962 by William B. Eerdmans Publishing Co. Used with permission. The stories
written by Gertrude Ann Priester are adapted from *Let's Talk about God,* © 1967 by the
Westminster Press. Used with permission. The stories written by Velma Kiefer are from
Stories to Tell in Children's Church, © 1966 by Baker Books. Used with permission. The
stories written by Dena Korfker are adapted from *Good Morning, Lord, Devotions for
Children,* © 1973 by Baker Book House Company. Used with permission. The stories
written by William C. Hendricks are adapted from *Good Morning, Lord, Devotions for
Boys,* © 1974 by Baker Book House Company. Used with permission. The story written
by Floyd and Pauline Todd is adapted from *Good Morning, Lord, Devotions for Campers,*
© 1973 by Baker Book House Company. Used with permission. The story written by
Greta Rey is adapted from *Good Morning, Lord, Devotions for Girls,* © 1975 by Baker
Book House Company. Used with permission.

Scripture is taken from the HOLY BIBLE, NEW INTERNATIONAL VERSION®. NIV®.
Copyright © 1973, 1978, 1984 by International Bible Society. Used by permission of
Zondervan Publishing House. All rights reserved.

For current information about all releases from Baker Book House, visit our web site:
http://www.bakerbooks.com

Contents

Preface

There's something special about a favorite book for reading when a child is ready to be tucked in for the night. And when the stories focus on familiar values and everyday events, children want to hear them again and again.

These stories, written by several master storytellers, wear well and can be read and re-read without boredom. Child and adult can talk about the events and behavior patterns. Several stories close with an appropriate prayer.

The vocabulary is designed to be read aloud to four- to seven-year-olds. Early readers will soon be reading favorite stories for themselves with only occasional help from an adult.

Sam Butcher's unique Precious Moments drawings with the large expressive eyes quickly convey joy, sadness, or humor. The soft, appealing colors attract both children and adults.

So the next time you hear, "I'm ready for a story now," pick up this happy combination of stories, prayers, and art. You and your child will not only be enjoying some very special minutes together, you will also be building some precious memories.

The Publishers

The Person inside You

When I Grow Up

Do you know what you want to be when you grow up? Maybe you have an uncle who is an airplane pilot and being able to fly a plane looks like fun to you. Maybe you have a cousin who is training to be an astronaut and you have decided to become one too. Some children are very good with pets. They love animals and seem to know just what to do when an animal needs help. They may grow up to be animal doctors.

But usually children don't have any idea what they want to be when they are grown. And that isn't a problem. Most children change their minds several times before they are ready for high school or college.

You will naturally choose something you are good at doing, something you know you will be able to do well. But if you are a Christian,

you will ask God to help you choose the right job for you. Then you will not only succeed in what you are doing, but you will please God at the same time.

So don't worry about what you are going to do. God knows how you will be able to serve him best. Just ask him to show you his plan as you grow older.

Dena Korfker

Let me live that I may praise you.

Psalm 119:175

I Want a Pet

Molly was going to be six in a few days.
Whenever anyone asked her what she
wanted for her birthday, she would say, "I
want a pet." Molly had had several small
pets in the past. She loved animals and
was always asking for another one.

She always promised to take good care of her pets. But Molly wasn't very good at keeping her promises. She would be very careful for the first few days. Then she would forget about taking care of her pet.

She left her turtle in the hot sun for a whole day. The water dried up in the pan, and her turtle died. Her bunnies were fun to have, and her mother warned her to watch them closely if she wanted to keep them. But, once again, Molly forgot. She left the door of the gate open one day, and the bunnies ran away. She never found them again.

But now that Molly was going to be six, she was begging for a new pet again. The

night before her birthday her dad was reading her the story of young David, the shepherd boy who took care of his father's sheep. When Molly's dad came to the part about the lion and the bear coming after the lamb, Molly's eyes grew big with wonder as she pictured the brave David rescuing his lamb from those fierce animals. Molly sighed, "I wish I could be as good with animals as David was."

"Now that you are going to be six," her dad said, "maybe you can remember to take care of a pet." So Molly got another pet. This time it was a kitten—the cutest little kitten you ever saw!

And Molly tried hard. She gave her kitten food and water every day. She played with it and snuggled with it whenever she had a chance. In fact, she never again forgot to take very good care of her pet.

Dena Korfker

*David went back and forth . . . to tend
his father's sheep at Bethlehem.*

1 Samuel 17:15

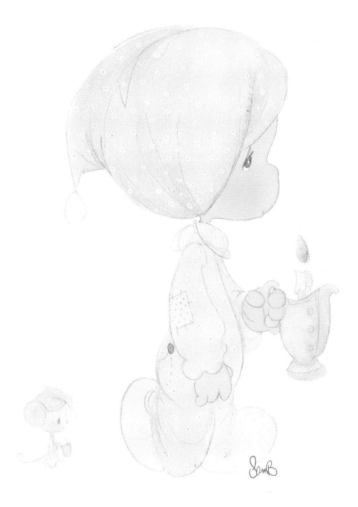

I Hate the Dark

Mother had called Travis three times to come and get ready for bed. Each time Travis had just one more thing that he *had* to do before he could come. Now Mother was impatient, and Travis knew that there could be no more excuses. He would *have* to go to bed!

Travis didn't mind the going to bed part. In fact, he was quite tired and had almost gone to sleep in the big chair in the family room after dinner. The part Travis didn't like was the darkness all around him.

When Travis was at home, his mother always left the little night-light burning just outside his door. But here at Aunt Jane's house, there was no night-light. Worst of all, Travis's bedroom was way down the hall from where Mother and Daddy were going to sleep. Travis was just plain afraid of the dark.

Travis slowly climbed the stairs to the bedroom where Mother was waiting. He washed his face and hands, put on his pajamas, and jumped into bed. Then he began to cry.

"Why, Travis, what's the matter?" asked Mother. "Don't you feel well? Tell me

about it." Mother sat down by the bed and felt to see if Travis had a fever.

Travis wiped his eyes and blinked back the tears. "I hate the dark!" he said. "I just hate it. I'm scared, Mother. Please let me sleep with the light on tonight."

Mother thought for a moment. Then she asked, "Travis, are you afraid of the sunshine?"

Travis looked puzzled. "Oh, Mother, of course not!" he said. "I love the sunshine."

22

Mother asked, "Are you afraid when the wind blows?"

"No," said Travis. "Well, I sort of am afraid when it blows too hard, but then I just come inside."

"Are you afraid of the rain or the snow?" asked Mother.

"I love to walk in the rain, and I love to play in the snow," answered Travis. "You always have to tell me not to get soaked, Mother."

"Alright," said Mother. "You love the sunshine, the wind, the rain, and the snow. You like to swim in the water and you like to climb on the mountains. Who do we believe made all these things, Travis?"

"Oh, I know that," said Travis. "It's God's world. He made the sun and the moon and the stars and everything. The sun shines and makes the day, and then it goes down and it gets dark and that's night. That's what I don't like!"

"God made the day and cares for us in it, and he also cares for us in the night," said Mother. "Both the day and the night are God's. The day is for working and playing. The night is for resting and sleeping. It takes both of them to make things right for people."

"I guess I didn't think much about the night being God's too," said Travis. "I was too busy hating it. I'll try, Mother. I'll say to myself, 'The night is God's also.'"

"There is a verse in the Bible that says the same thing," said Mother. "It says, 'Yours is the day, yours also is the night.' I'll show you where to find it in the morning and you can read it for yourself. Good night now, Travis. It's time for your bedtime prayer."

Gertrude Ann Priester

Thank you, God,
for day and night.
You care for us in the daytime,
when we can see all about us,
and we know that you also care for us
during the night,
when it is dark and we cannot see.
Thank you that the darkness
does not hide us from you.
Thank you for your love and care
that are the same day and night.
Amen.

Running to Win

It's fun to run with your friends to see who can run the fastest. Maybe sometimes you win, but other times your friends win.

When champion runners enter a race, they aren't running just for fun; they want to win the prize. Does everyone get a prize? No, only the one who runs the fastest. Then why try, if you aren't sure that you will be the winner? That isn't the way champions talk, is it? They do not know if they will win the prize, but they want that prize, and they are going to try their very hardest to make sure they get it. When Jesus lived on earth, people ran races with lightning-fast horses and chariots. The men who took part in these races would stand in their two-wheeled wagons and guide their horses around the track. Sometimes these men wanted to win so badly that they would not obey

28

all the rules. They would put sharp spears on the wheels of their chariots and then run so close to the other chariots that their spinning spears would break the wheels of those chariots. The other charioteer would be thrown from his chariot and would be unable to continue the race.

One of the men who wrote many of the books in the Bible knew about those unfair races. His name was Paul. He also knew about the races where a man ran a course to win a prize. Maybe Paul sat in the great stadiums of that day and watched some of those races.

Paul thought of his own life as a race. He worked as hard as he could. He did the very best he knew how to do. And he kept his eye on the goal, which was heaven.

When Paul's life was almost over, he said, "I have fought the good fight, I have finished the race, I have kept the faith." There was no laziness for Paul, no unfair fighting, and no cheating. Paul did his best, and he was satisfied.

How about you? Did you do your best today? If you didn't, maybe you could promise God that you will try harder tomorrow.

Dena Korfker

Forgetting what is behind
and straining toward
what is ahead,
I press on toward the goal
to win the prize.

Philippians 3:13–14

Watch Your Tongue

Parrots are colorful birds. Their red, yellow, green, and blue feathers and their loud squawks make the parrot cages at the zoo favorite spots. Have you ever heard a parrot say, "Hi!" or ask, "How are you today?"

A parrot can only repeat what someone else has taught it to say because it doesn't think for itself. It doesn't know whether the words it repeats are good or bad.

When one young boy was asked why he had said something he shouldn't have, he answered, "I didn't say it, my tongue did."

But people aren't parrots. People can think and express their thoughts with words. So we are responsible for everything we say. Matthew 12:36 reminds us that when Jesus comes back to earth, we will have to explain all the mean and careless things we have said.

Be sure your words are pleasing to God. Don't be a parrot!

William C. Hendricks

I will watch my ways and keep my tongue from sin.

Psalm 39:1

Count Your Blessings

Do you ever look at your friends' stuff and think, "Their stuff is much better than mine"? Do you always have to make sure that your piece of cake is just as big as your brother's or sister's?

It is so easy to feel sorry for ourselves, isn't it? Often we think we're not getting our fair share. That is something every Christian has to fight every day. Even fathers and mothers feel sorry for themselves at times. But that isn't a good thing to do.

Often what we tell ourselves when we feel unhappy is not true. We tend to make things sound worse than they really are.

Perhaps another girl's sweater is prettier than yours and you wish you had that sweater. You might say to your mother, "Every girl in my class dresses better than I do."

Or maybe your friend's dad took him to a ball game and you're jealous. So you tell your dad, "I'm the only boy in my class who can't go to the ball game with his dad."

When we feel sorry for ourselves, we make ourselves miserable, and we usually make everyone else feel miserable too!

I know a song called "Count Your Blessings." Have you ever tried to do just that?

Do you think you don't have any blessings? Think again. Use your fingers to count all the blessings you can think of. The more you think, the longer your list will grow. Soon you will have more blessings than fingers.

What will the blessings on your list be? A family who loves you. A good home. Two eyes to see. Two good legs to carry you where you want to go. Don't stop there, though. Keep on going.

When that old "feeling-sorry-for-yourself" mood starts to bother you again, count some of your blessings. Soon that sad feeling will disappear, and a big smile will take its place.

Dena Korfker

And my God will meet all your needs according to his glorious riches in Christ Jesus.

Philippians 4:19

The People beside You

No One Listens

Kristin and Brian each had a dollar they had earned by delivering notices of a neighborhood meeting to all the houses on their block. They had decided to put their money together to buy a kite. "We can take turns flying it," they said. "It's better to buy one kite together than to wait until we could earn this much more money."

They went to the store and found the counter where the kites were on display. The sign said, KITES—$2 EACH. Kristin looked at her money and Brian looked at his money. Together it made two dollars. "We would like to buy a kite, please," said Kristin.

"Do you have money?" asked the clerk.

"I have a dollar," said Kristin.

"And I have—" began Brian. But the clerk wasn't listening. "Kites are two dollars, little girl. You don't have enough money." And he walked away to take care of another customer.

"I have some money too," called Brian. But the clerk only shook his head and waved at them to go away and not bother him.

When the children got home, Brian went to look for their father. "Dad! Where are you? Will you help Kristin and me buy a kite?" he called.

Dad was busy down in the basement. "I think you have spent enough money this week, Brian. You'll have to buy it with your own money if you want a kite."

"But, Dad, I *have* the money . . . or Kristin and I do to-gether," said Brian.

"Please don't keep pestering me, Brian," said Dad. "I'm very busy right now. You know what I said about giving you more money."

Brian looked at Kristin. "Just like that man in the store! He won't listen to us either!"

That night when Kristin was saying her prayers, she stopped suddenly. "What's the matter?" asked Mother. "You didn't finish your prayers."

"Well, maybe I won't finish them," said Kristin. "If God is like that man in the store or like Dad when he's busy in the basement, what's the use of praying? Maybe God won't listen either!"

After Mother heard all of the story, she said, "Often grown-ups have a bad habit of not really listening carefully to children. Sometimes it's just because we're busy. Some- times we

44

think we know what they are going to say before they say it—and that is wrong. But God is never too busy, and he always wants to know our thoughts and feelings. It does not matter how old you are when you pray to God—he listens to everyone! God wants you to come to him to give praise and thanks, to ask for his help, and to tell him whatever you want to say. Don't ever think that he is not listening, Kristin."

Mother opened the Bible and read a verse from Mark 10 to her: "Let the little children come to me, and do not hinder them, for the kingdom of heaven belongs to such as these."

Kristin's mother was right. God calls children to him, just as he calls people of all ages. When you forget this sometimes and think that maybe you should not bother to pray because you think God might not listen, remember the verse that Kristin learned. You can find it in your Bible in Mark 10:14.

Gertrude Ann Priester

Dear God,
you love little children
and big people too. 
Thank you
for always listening to us
when we pray.
Help us to trust you,
and to know that you will never
send us away
because you are too busy
or too tired to listen to us.
Thank you
for your love,
and for hearing and answering
prayers.
Amen.

46

The Artist Who Forgot
Four Colors

Once there was an artist who was asked
to paint a large picture or mural for a
new church. The church was called The
Church of the Christ Child, so the people

wanted him to paint a picture that had children in it.

The artist painted a picture on a large white canvas. He made a lovely picture of Jesus with many children crowding around him. The children looked so happy that it made the artist happy to look at them. He could hardly wait for the people from the church to come the next morning to give their approval.

But after he was in his bed that night, he dreamed that he heard someone moving near the picture. He ran to look. There was a stranger painting on his picture! "Stop, stop!" the artist cried. "You are spoiling my picture!"

The stranger turned to him and calmly said, "I am just making it right. Why did you use only one of your five colors for the faces of the children?"

The artist stammered. "I—I—just never thought about it."

The stranger smiled. "Well, I have made some of the faces yellow, some brown, some black, and some red; for these little ones have come from many lands in answer to my call."

"Your call?" asked the artist. "What call was that, Sir?"

"Let the little children come to me, and do not stop them, for they are part of the kingdom of heaven," the stranger said.

Suddenly the stranger was gone and the artist awoke to find himself still in his bed. He rushed to his picture and began to paint furiously. Quickly he painted many new faces using *all* of his colors.

Now the children came from every land in the world: some were Asian, some African, some Indian. The picture was better than any the artist had ever painted. And the people were very pleased with it.

One lady said, "Why, it's God's family at home with him, isn't it?"

Are you a part of God's big family?

Dena Korfker

Dear friends, now we are
children of God.

1 John 3:2

Teamwork Wins

Some people think football is a great sport. The players must be in good shape so their muscles can work well. The runner must be able to decide quickly if he should turn right or left. The quarterback must call out directions and throw the ball to the right spot. The blocker must keep the other team away from the ball.

Planning the moves of the next play and making them work is really exciting. A single football player couldn't win the game without the rest of the team. The blockers open the way for the player who is carrying the ball; one player passes, another receives the pass. It's teamwork that wins the football game. The work of Christians in God's kingdom is a lot like playing a football game. When Christians gather together on Sunday to worship and praise God, they build up God's team. They listen to God's plan being explained through the preaching of the Bible. The team members get directions for passing the love of Jesus to others. Each member has a job to do and the members help each other to be strong Christians.

Are you a good member of God's team?

William C. Hendricks

Now you are the body of Christ, and each of you is a part of it.

1 Corinthians 12:27

Give Away

"Give," said the little stream
As it hurried down the hill.
"I'm small, I know, but wherever I go
The trees grow greener still.
Singing, singing all the day,
Give, oh, give away."

This song tells us something about God's world. The streams give water where it is needed. The trees keep the ground from washing away with the rains. The sun warms everything that grows.

We could not live without the gifts God gave us. Our life is a gift of God. God gives us our growth, our health, our minds. Everything we have comes from God.

Is it hard for you to say "Thank you"? Is it hard for you to share? Is it hard for you to give things away?

Every year our country sets aside a special day for giving thanks. We call it Thanksgiving Day. On that day God's people go to church and bring gifts to share with people who need food, clothes, homes, money, or medicine. That's one way to show thanks to God. Can you think of another way to thank God? That's right—say a big THANK YOU, GOD! now for the blessings he has given you.

Make every day a THANK YOU, GOD! day. Ask yourself each night before you go to sleep, "What did I give away today?" Maybe you gave your time to help someone who couldn't finish a job alone. Or maybe you let your brother or sister play with your favorite toy. Now thank God for the things he gives to you.

Dena Korfker

God loves a cheerful giver.

2 Corinthians 9:7

A Surprise for Mother

"Hey, Dan!" whispered Megan to her younger brother. "I know what we can do."

"Huh, do what?" asked Dan loudly, glancing up from his book.

"Shh-h, Mother will hear us," warned Megan. "I said, 'I know what we can do.'"

"Do about what?"

"You know," answered Megan in an impatient whisper.

Dan frowned. "I don't—" But the frown turned into a grin. "Oh, yeah, I forgot—Sunday."

"I just heard Mother tell Dad she has to go to see Mrs. Walsh tonight," said Megan. "We can make our Mother's Day gifts while she's gone. Okay?" Dan nodded.

As soon as Mother was gone, Megan got two sheets of white paper and pencils and crayons. She put them on the kitchen table. Then she explained, "I'm going to make a card like Miss Taylor showed us in school today. First I have to fold the paper in half. Like this.

"Then I'll fold it in half again. Miss Taylor says this is a French fold. It's like the cards we buy in the store.

"Now I can draw a picture on the outside and color it. Or I can cut out a picture and paste it on the cover." Megan began to draw a picture on the cover of her card.

Dan decided to make a heart-shaped card. He folded his piece of paper in half and drew one side of a heart. Then he carefully cut out the heart and unfolded his card. Then he took a crayon and drew a border on it.

Soon Dan and Megan had finished the covers of their cards. And on each one they neatly printed two words: TO MOTHER.

"But I don't see what's so won-derful about making our own cards for Mother on Mother's Day," said Dan, looking disap-pointed.

"It isn't the card that's special," said

To Mother

Megan. "It's the gift we'll put inside." She opened her card. "On the inside we will write our gifts to Mother. We will each give her a gift of ourselves. Like, I'll write in my card, *Dear Mother, I give you my hands to make your bed and my bed every morning for two weeks. And I give my hands to clear the table after dinner without grumbling. With love, Megan.* See? You can write a gift for Mother too. Something to help her or make her glad."

"I get it." Dan scratched his head thoughtfully. "But what can I give? I know. I'll write, *Dear Mother, I give you my feet to run and get things for you. And I give my hands to make my bed so you won't need to.*"

Carefully Dan and Megan wrote their gifts. Quickly they tucked their cards into envelopes and hid them in secret places until Sunday. They couldn't wait to see

Mother's surprise and joy when she opened her Mother's Day gifts.

Have you been wishing for a special Mother's Day gift for your mother? Would you like to give her a gift of yourself, as Megan and Dan did?

Velma Kiefer

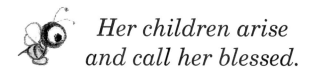 *Her children arise and call her blessed.*

Proverbs 31:28

The Day with No End

Mark woke up so early that no one else in the whole house heard him tiptoe to the window and look out to see what kind of day it was. It had been raining hard last night when Mark went to sleep, but now the rain had almost stopped and Mark saw the sun shining on the red bricks of the house across the street. When he looked up into the blue sky he saw a beautiful rainbow that stretched from one end of the sky to the other. The treetops and flowers glistened in the sunshine, and it looked like a day that would be perfect for riding his bike, eating a picnic on the grassy field with his family, and playing ball. He saw a day that was just exactly what a holiday should be.

Mark waited patiently for the rest of his family to wake up. After everyone had eaten some breakfast, Mark decided to ride his bike and see how many of his friends were going to be in the parade that afternoon.

Every child in the neighborhood could decorate their bike or wagon or tricycle and ride around the big circle of road when the little band began to play. Mark

joined some of his friends who were cutting paper streamers and taping them to their bike wheels and handlebars. He decided to use blue crepe paper with some green strips that would fly out in the wind as he rode.

Before Mark knew it, Mother was calling him for lunch: a peanut butter sandwich and chocolate milk with a chocolate brownie for dessert! What a day this was!

Next came the parade, with everybody laughing and clapping and taking pictures of the bikes and wagons and anything that would go on wheels. It was fun to be one of the older children who did not have to ride slowly in a line so that no one would get bumped. It was fun not to be treated like a little kid.

Then there was a program of singing and games in the big field beside the road. Friends who had not seen each other for several weeks visited and exchanged sto-

ries. Little children tumbled over their older brothers and sisters. Parents watched their babies play on blankets in the sunshine. Everyone did just what he or she pleased. It was great fun!

Best of all was the community picnic where each family put a dish of food on a long table set up at the edge of the field. Mark took his plate and got in line, sniffing the good smells from up ahead. Soon he had a plate full of good things to eat—even more chocolate brownies!

The children started a baseball game, and Mark hit a home run his first time up at bat. Everyone was calling him "heavy hitter" and he felt almost like the star of the game.

And then it was time to go home and get ready for bed. "I wish," said Mark, "that today would not end!"

His mother brought him some clean pajamas and sent him off to take a shower. When Mark was ready to climb into bed, Mother said, "Listen while I read what the Bible has to say about a day that would never end. 'There is a time for everything, and a season for every activity under heaven. . . . He has made everything beautiful in its time.'"

Mark snuggled under the covers. "I guess I'd get tired riding a bike or playing ball forever. And I'd get sick if I kept on eating the way I did at the picnic. Anyway, it feels good to be in this bed, because I'm tired, Mother."

"There's a time to play and a time to sleep," said Mother as she tucked Mark in and turned out the light. "A time to work and a time to sleep. Things are good when they are done in their proper time."

Gertrude Ann Priester

Thank you, God, for days
when we can work and play,
and for nights when we can sleep.
Thank you for making everything
good and beautiful
in its time.
Amen.

The God above You

Hello, God

Lisa crumpled up the piece of paper on which she had been writing and threw it at the wastebasket. It missed! Several others had missed also, and the floor around the basket was cluttered with crumpled paper.

"Hi!" said Lisa's big brother, Rob, as he came into the room to look for his history book. "Are you going out for basketball? You'll never make it by the looks of that mess!"

"Oh, pooh!" said Lisa. "Go away. I'm writing something."

Rob kicked at the papers. "Writing? There's nothing much on these papers." He smoothed out several sheets and read, "'A Prayer,' 'Dear God,' and 'For all the things . . .'"

Lisa groaned. "We're supposed to write a prayer that sounds as though we are just talking to God. Not some long thing with a lot of words like *bless* and *merciful* and stuff like that. It's supposed to be something we want to say to God. I don't know how to start."

Rob flopped into the big chair beside his sister. "That shouldn't be too hard," he said. "Let's see. Think for a minute about what God is like. You know, if you ask Mother for something, you just go right to her and say what you want because you know she will listen and pay attention to you."

"And if I ask that grumpy old man in the toy store something, I know he'll growl at me. So mostly I don't ask him. I always get someone else to do it!" laughed Lisa.

"You get the idea," said Rob. "Now, what is God like? That comes first."

"Well," said Lisa, thinking very hard, "I think he wants me to come to him, so I think he won't mind listening. He won't say he's too busy, or anything like that. And I can say whatever I want, because he won't get mad and stop loving me. I know that! So I'm not afraid.

And I guess God likes to know that I am thankful and glad for things he does for us, so he wants me to tell him that too."

"It sounds as though you were going to talk to a friend!" said Rob. "Now you should think about *why* you are praying to God. Any ideas?"

"Oh, sure," said Lisa. "I want to! I wouldn't like it if I thought I couldn't pray to God, especially when I need help! I guess sometimes I pray because I think I should—and sometimes because everyone else is praying, like in church or at the table, or something."

"You said before that you prayed because God wanted you to," said Rob.

"And because I *need* to," said Lisa. "You can't get along on your own all the time, so you need to ask for God's help."

"I think you also *need* to say thank you," said Rob. "People who never say thanks miss a lot."

"Maybe I should start writing now," said Lisa. "I want to get finished before I have to take my piano lesson."

"Well, think about what you have just told me. God is loving and kind and you know he is waiting to hear your prayers. You want to go to him to tell him about a lot of things. If God were someone you could see and touch, like Mother or Daddy or a favorite friend, what would you say to him?"

Lisa waited a minute before she answered. Then she grinned and said, "I think I'd just say, 'Hello, God!'"

Gertrude Ann Priester

Hello, God!
I want to tell you
that I think the spring
[or fall or summer
or winter] days
we are having are wonderful.
Thank you
for making such a beautiful world.

I'd also like to say that
I had a hard time today
being nice to _____
and I need your help
so that I can do better tomorrow.
There are some things
that have happened to my family
that I don't understand,
and I just want to tell you
that I have a little trouble
trusting that you will care for us all.
But I really do trust you!
I guess it's just that I don't understand
the way you do things.
I also want to say
thank you a million times
for all the love I get
from my mother
and father,
and lots of other people—
and from you.
Amen.

Clean Hands

If you were playing football or soccer and your parents called you home for dinner, one of them might say, "Be sure to wash your hands before you come to the table." If the playing field was wet and muddy, they might insist that you take a bath or shower.

Tiny babies and patients in a hospital are given a bath every morning. Many of us take a shower every day.

Why all this worry about a little dirt? What's so important about being clean?

When the microscope was invented, many germs could be seen for the first time. Today scientists are learning about germs that are so small you can't see them with even the best microscope. Germs that make people sick grow very fast in dirt. That's why it's so important to get rid of the dirt on our bodies.

When the Bible talks about "clean hands," it is talking about a different way to be clean. Sin is like dirt that we need to wash away. When we do wrong things and sin covers our lives like dirt, we must ask God to forgive us. He will help us keep our hands from doing wrong things.

William C. Hendricks

*Those with clean hands
will grow stronger.*

Job 17:9

85

The Slug

Jacob and Jeremy looked at the bubble-gum machine in the back corner of Mr. Swanson's store.

"Wish we had a penny," sighed Jacob, staring at the rainbow-colored balls.

"How about the one you found yesterday?" asked Jeremy.

"It's not a real penny," explained Jacob. He reached into his pocket, got out the slug, and held it up for Jeremy to see. "See, it's only a piece of metal that looks like a penny. It's a slug."

"Hey, why don't we put it into the machine and see what happens?" suggested Jeremy. "If it works we'll get some gum. Mr. Swanson won't know who put it in."

Jacob looked at the slug again. *That wouldn't be honest. It would be stealing,* said a voice inside him.

But quickly he stuck the piece of metal into the slot and turned the crank. Nineteen gumballs came rushing out, spilling all over the ground. The boys grinned at each other in surprise and scooped up the colored balls.

Jacob gave Jeremy a red one. He popped a blue one into his mouth. The others they dropped into their pockets. Their pockets bulging, the boys left the store. Slowly they walked up the street to Dan's house to play.

Jacob forgot all about the slug until bedtime. When he knelt to pray, he suddenly remembered. The voice inside said, *You should not steal.* Jacob squirmed. He pretended he had not heard the words. But they came again, *You should not steal, you should not steal.*

The voice bothered Jacob so much he decided not to pray. He jumped into bed and pulled the covers over his head. Would the covers shut out the words he didn't want to hear? No, they were still there. Jacob tossed and turned this way and that. He couldn't sleep. At last he sat up in bed in the darkness. Softly he prayed, "Dear God, I'm sorry I put the slug in Mr. Swanson's machine. I know it was wrong. Forgive me. Help me never to steal anything again. Amen."

Jacob lay down. He felt better. But then it seemed as if God said, "I forgive you, Jacob. But now you must pay Mr. Swanson what you owe him."

I'd be ashamed to, thought Jacob. *I'd have to tell him what I did . . . I can't do that.* But he knew he should do it, no matter how hard it would be.

"I'll go tell Mr. Swanson first thing in the morning," he promised. "And I'll pay him on Saturday when I get my allowance." Then he fell asleep.

In the morning Jacob didn't forget. He asked Jesus to help him, and as soon as the store was open, Jacob went in. It wasn't as hard as he thought it would be

to tell what he had done. Mr. Swanson stuck his hands into his two back pockets as he listened to Jacob. "Why did you come and tell me?" he asked, raising his bushy brows.

"Well, because I'm a Christian and stealing is wrong. God made me sorry. He wanted me to tell you and pay you."

Mr. Swanson nodded. "I'm glad you told me. You make me wish I were a Christian too."

Velma Kiefer

*The Lord our God is merciful
and forgiving,
even though we have
rebelled against him.*

Daniel 9:9

The Lost Sheep

Have you ever seen a shepherd taking care of his sheep? Many children living in America never see a shepherd. But in the land where Jesus lived, it was a very common sight. Even today there are many,

many shepherds leading their sheep on the steep hills in that country.

When Jesus wanted the people to understand how much he loved his own people, he told them a story about a lost sheep.

A shepherd had a hundred sheep. And this shepherd knew every one of those sheep. He even gave them names. When he called them by name, the sheep would come running.

All day long the shepherd would lead his sheep. He brought them to a good place to eat grass and he brought them to quiet streams of water so they could drink their fill. He led them up steep hills to find more grass and let them rest in a shady place. And when night

came, he would bring them back to the sheepfold. Each night he counted his sheep to make sure they were all there.

One night the count was short. There were only ninety-nine sheep. One was gone. But why bother about one little sheep? The shepherd was tired. He had had a long day. But he couldn't forget about that one missing sheep. It didn't matter to him that he had ninety-nine sheep safe in the sheepfold. It didn't matter that the weather was getting stormy or that it would be very hard to see in the dark. He just had to find that one sheep. He loved that sheep.

So the shepherd went out into the storm and began to look for the sheep. Up and down the hills he went, calling and calling. Finally, between loud thunder crashes, he heard a faint "Baa-Baa!" And in the flash of the lightning he saw his sheep, caught in the bushes.

The shepherd ran to get the lost sheep. Carefully he carried the little animal home. How the shepherd loved that sheep!

And what did Jesus say about this story? He said that he was the Good Shepherd who loves us, his sheep. Then he said, "The angels in heaven shout for joy when one of my little ones comes to me." Are you one of the little ones that Jesus loves?

Dena Korfker

I am the good shepherd.

John 10:11

I Wish

Amy and Andy were tired. They were grumpy too. In fact, they were so tired and grumpy that their mother stopped ironing, sat down on the couch, and called the twins to come and join her. Mother knew that it was a good thing to stop trouble *before* it started!

"I wish," said Amy.

"I wish," said Andy.

". . . that tomorrow was Christmas!" they both said.

Mother laughed. "So that's it! Too much waiting for Christmas. I wonder though . . . are both of you *ready* for Christmas?"

The twins nodded their heads. "Oh, yes," said Andy. "I made up the list of things I want a long time ago. And I got a model kit for Brad, because he's giving me a snap-together station for my train set. I got a couple of other things too. Oh, I'm ready!"

"I'm ready too," agreed Amy. "I finished all my shopping a week ago. All the parties are done already, and we hurried and went caroling early so everyone wouldn't be bored listening to the same old songs that every group sings."

"So now you wish that tomorrow was Christmas," said Mother. "Well, now let's see . . . *I* wish too."

"What's your wish?" asked Andy.

"Are you wishing you will get the new sewing machine you want?" asked Amy.

"No," answered Mother. "I wish that everyone would stop hurrying around *doing* so many things and would take time to *think* about Christmas. I wish everyone would get ready to celebrate what Christmas is really all about!"

"But Christmas is about Jesus being born, isn't it?" asked Amy.

"It's about the shepherds coming to the stable to see the baby Jesus," said Andy.

"Yes, it's about all that," said Mother. "But it is *more!* It is being happy and thankful that the baby who was born was not just another child coming into the world, important as that is. It is celebrating the coming of God's own Son, who shows us and tells us that God's love is the greatest gift of our whole life."

"That's so hard to understand," said Andy. "I wish I could have been with the wisemen when they followed the star to Bethlehem!"

"I wish I knew why Jesus had to be born in a stable," Amy added.

"That's why we all need to

take time to get *ready* for Christmas," said Mother. "We need to try to understand better what we are celebrating. Let's play a game. It's called 'I Wish'—with wishes that would help us to be truly ready."

"Okay," said Andy. "I wish that I could have stood out in the field with the shepherds and heard the angels singing about 'Glory in the highest.' I wonder if I would have been scared."

Amy thought for a moment. "I wish that I could have seen Mary holding the baby Jesus for the first time. I wish I knew what she was thinking about when she laid him in the manger."

Mother said, "I wish I knew what Mary and Joseph thought about Jesus. Did they talk about why this child had been born to them

and how they would bring him up to please God?"

"Let's start reading a little part of the Christmas story every day, and then we can talk about it," said Amy.

"Sure," said Andy. "We hear the whole thing so often we don't even really listen anymore. Let's pretend we are the people who were there and see how we think we would feel about everything that happened."

"All right," said Mother. "We'll start right now with the beginning of Luke 2 where it tells about Mary and Joseph traveling to Bethlehem. Will you bring me the Bible, Andy? I'll read just a few verses to get us started."

Gertrude Ann Priester

Thank you, God,
that you love us so much
that you sent your Son
to show us your great love.

We know that you have always been
faithful
in keeping your promises
to your people.
Thank you
that Christmas is
more than celebrating
a baby's birthday.
Thank you
that it is
celebrating
your gift of love
to us.
Amen

Jesus Came from Heaven

Each year you have a birthday, and then you think of the day you were born. You were a tiny baby then, a very *dear* little baby.

Jesus was born a tiny baby too. But Jesus did not *begin* to live when he was born. Long, long before the earth was made, Jesus lived in heaven with God the Father and God the Holy Spirit.

You remember that the earth was all good and beautiful at first. Adam and Eve were wonderful; they were made in God's likeness. But sin came and spoiled everything.

God felt sorry about the sorrow and trouble that came after that. And he said, "We will send a Savior."

God sent Jesus, his Son, to be the Savior. Jesus was given a human body and was born a little baby in Bethlehem.

Oh, how the angels sang that night—a great host of angels! They were so glad that Jesus had gone down to earth. They were glad because he went to be our Savior.

What a change it was for Jesus to come down from heaven to earth! Heaven is full of glory. There is no sickness there, nor sadness or sin. But Jesus left his beautiful home, and his father, and the wonderful angels, to come down to our sinful earth.

Jesus was rich in heaven; everything was his. When he came to earth, he was poor. He left all his riches and glory behind. There was not even a house ready for him on earth. He was born in a stable. And he did not have a bed. His mother, Mary, had to lay him in a manger.

Jesus was almighty in heaven. He was the Lord of heaven and earth, and Lord over the angels.

When he became a baby, he could not do anything! Babies need a mother to take care of them. Jesus was helpless, like all other babies.

Jesus became just like us, except that he had no sin in his heart.

The story of Jesus' birth is the most wonderful story in the Bible. It is the most wonderful story in all the world and the most wonderful story in heaven. Just think of it—Jesus, the Son of God, became a baby!

He became a baby to be our Savior, because God loves us so much and wanted to save us.

Marian Schoolland

Though he was rich,
yet for your sakes
he became poor.

2 Corinthians 8:9

The World around You

Thank You for Common Things

Good night, Lord. This day wasn't a special day, but it was a good day. I don't have any problems to talk about tonight and I feel happy.

Usually, Lord, I thank you for important things; but tonight I want to thank you for common things. I'll add more to the list as I think about them before I go to sleep.

Thank you for:

rain
buzzing bees
the wind
fishing poles
pretty stones
green trees and
  blue sky
shadows and lights
smooth sheets on
  my bed

school buses on
  rainy days
parents to fix our
  lunches
pens and markers
birds in the winter
  time
my sense of smell
good ideas

Amen.

Greta Rey

God . . . richly provides us with everything for our enjoyment.

1 Timothy 6:17

112

Time

Isn't time wonderful? It is one of the best gifts God gave us. We would not know how to live without time. We would not know when to get up, or when to go to school, or when to eat if there were no time. The farmer wouldn't know when it was spring and time to plant, or when it was fall and time to harvest. We would not be able to make any plans. How could we plan meetings, or picnics, or camping trips if we didn't know about time?

When God made the sun and the moon, he made time too. He planned for days and nights, for winter and summer, for worktime and playtime.

God has shown us how to break up time into smaller parts too. The days are divided into hours and minutes and seconds. Seconds are very short. Just count to one and a second is gone. Minutes aren't much longer. Count to sixty slowly and a minute has gone by. There are sixty counts, or seconds, in a minute; and there are sixty minutes in an hour. Hours make up days and nights. And so time goes on— as long as this world lasts.

Maybe your mom or dad will let you see a minute go by on their watch. Have you thanked God for the gift of time? Now is a good time to do that.

Dena Korfker

My times are in your hands.

Psalm 31:15

Snow

Do you like to play in the snow? Do you like to catch snowflakes on your tongue? Have you ever seen two snowflakes that look exactly alike?

Snow is so beautiful. It comes down so softly. It is fun to watch it glide gracefully through the sky. And snow does such a good job of covering up a dirty world. It's so much fun to play in the snow, to slide on it, or to make a snowman, or maybe a fort.

Snow is just as beautiful at night as it is in the daytime. With the help of street lights or the moon, the snow dresses the trees and the shrubs in sparkling jewels. And the evergreen trees look lovely in their fluffy white coats.

Sometimes people can make fake snow. But that costs many dollars and it takes lots of time. It takes a long time to make enough snow just to cover one ski hill. But God can cover a whole city, or even many cities, with a thick blanket of snow in just a little time.

And none of the snowflakes are alike. Try to catch one on your mitten the next time it is snowing. Then catch another one. Can you see how each one is different? But God made each one of them.

God made people different too. Among the millions and millions of people in the world, none of them is alike. There is nobody in the world exactly like you. Thank God now for making snowflakes. Then, thank him for making people. You can give him a special thank you because you are one of a kind and very special.

Dena Korfker

He says to the snow,
"Fall on the earth."

Job 37:6

Sand Castles

One afternoon Jill and Joey built what they thought was the finest sand castle ever. They worked long and hard. When it was finished they were so proud. They had never seen such a beautiful sand castle. Even the gate around the castle was just right. They took one last look at it and went back to the campground for dinner and a campfire sing-along.

During the night the wind and the waves leveled the beautiful castle. In the morning there was only smooth, wet sand—not even a lump where the castle had been.

Sand is great for building sand castles. But we want tougher materials when we build our lives. Paul, a man who wrote many books in the Bible, said that prayer and reading the Bible and doing good to others are the right materials to use when we build our lives. Paul wanted us to trust Jesus so that our lives would be strong and beautiful. Use some good materials each day so that you will grow spiritually.

Floyd and Pauline Todd

Everyone who hears these words of mine . . . is like a wise man who built his house on the rock.

Matthew 7:24

Shadows

Were you afraid of shadows when you were small? Are you still afraid of shadows? I know a fun story about a little boy who was very afraid of the dark. His name was Nathan.

One night when Nathan's mother and father were downstairs and he was asleep in his bed, the moon came out, the wind rattled the shutters outside his window, and Nathan woke up. He looked around

at all the dark shadows in his room and screamed. He was so-o-o-o frightened! Before Nathan's mother and father could come upstairs, Alexander, his dog, quickly came to his side.

"What's the matter?" Alexander seemed to ask as he tilted his furry head and looked up at Nathan.

"Wild animals!!!" cried Nathan. "My room is FULL of them! I see a tiger, and a rhinoceros, and a gorilla, and a huge snake all curled up!"

Quickly Nathan reached for the flashlight his mom kept beside his bed and he and Alexander shone the light on all the wild animals. To Nathan's great surprise, the tiger was his striped chair, the huge rhino was his bookcase, the gorilla was the light fixture hanging from the ceiling, and the snake all curled up beside his bed was Nathan's clothing lying on the floor where he had left it. Nathan laughed with

Alexander and promised never to be afraid in the dark again.

Some shadows are very beautiful. They add much to the beauty of God's great world. Have you ever sat in the shadow of a big tree on a hot day? Have you ever watched your own shadow as you ran down the street? Sometimes shadows are long and sometimes shadows are dark.

Many times shadows are made by ordinary things, and people only imagine that they are dangerous. Remember, it takes a light to make a shadow. With a stronger light you can chase shadows away and see what made them.

Are you still afraid of night shadows? Well, keep a flashlight handy, and ask God to help you to be brave.

Dena Korfker

 When I am afraid,
I will trust in you.

Psalm 56:3